W9-AAW-574

Disney · PIXAR

TOY STORY

A Roaring Adventure

By Kristen L. Depken
Illustrated by Josh Holtsclaw

A GOLDEN BOOK • NEW YORK

Copyright © 2012 Disney/Pixar. All rights reserved. Published in the United States by Golden Books, an imprint of Random House Children's Books, a division of Random House, Inc., 1745 Broadway, New York, NY 10019, and in Canada by Random House of Canada Limited, Toronto, in conjunction with Disney Enterprises, Inc. Golden Books, A Golden Book, A Little Golden Book, the G colophon, and the distinctive gold spine are registered trademarks of Random House, Inc.
ISBN: 978-0-7364-2907-8
randomhouse.com/kids
Printed in the United States of America
10 9 8 7 6 5 4 3 2 1

Bonnie's toys were putting on a play about dinosaurs. Mr. Pricklepants was the director. Buzz and Woody were building the set. Trixie was in charge of costumes.

Rex was auditioning for the part of King of the Jungle— the **biggest, strongest** dinosaur.

"Give me your loudest roar," Mr. Pricklepants told Rex.

Rex took a deep breath and let out his biggest **roar.**

It was barely more than a squeak.

Mr. Pricklepants shook his head. "Sorry, Rex," he said. "But you've got to believe it to be it."

ROOaarrr

"Don't worry," Woody told Rex. "I'm sure there's another job for you."

But Rex wasn't listening. "I'm the only dinosaur who can't roar!" he cried. He trudged off to Bonnie's closet and fell fast asleep.

Rex soon began to dream that he was in a jungle filled with thick vines, dark leaves, and a giant smoking volcano. He could hear dinosaurs **roaring** in the distance.

Suddenly, a **giant** bird swooped down. Rex turned to run—and stepped right into a trap!

It quickly pulled him up into the air. **"Help!"** he cried.

A tribe of cave-Aliens
came running.

"I'm a friend!" yelled Rex.

"Sorry," said Mr.
Pricklepants, the leader of the
cave-Aliens. "We're trying to
capture the King of the
Jungle. He's a **big,** mean
dinosaur who won't
leave us alone."

Just then, the bird swooped down again—it was Buzz
on a giant glider! Woody swung down from a nearby tree.
They wanted to capture the King of the Jungle, too.
"Will you help us?" Buzz asked Rex.

"I bet your roar could scare the King of the Jungle away," said Trixie. "Let's hear it."

Rex looked around nervously, then took a deep breath.

A huge **roar** rumbled through the jungle.

"See, I told you!" said Trixie.

"That wasn't me!" cried Rex.

An enormous **T. rex** burst through the trees!
"The King of the Jungle!" cried the cave-Aliens.
"Roar, Rex!" said Trixie. "Scare him away!"

Rex tried to roar, but all that came out was a measly **squeak**. The giant dinosaur laughed and laughed.

When a cave-Alien threw a rock at the mean dinosaur, the King of the Jungle scooped up the Alien and ran toward the volcano.

"Not so fast, you big lizard!" shouted Buzz. He swooped down in his jungle glider, but the King of the Jungle swatted him away.

Woody tried to lasso the
dinosaur, but the King of the
Jungle broke through the ropes
and kept running.
Buzz and Woody raced
after the mean
dinosaur. Rex and
the rest of their
friends followed
close behind.

Near the volcano, Mr. Pricklepants told everyone what to do. "Buzz, use your laser. Woody, use your lasso." Then he turned to Rex. "You have to use your roar."

"But my roar isn't big enough," said Rex.

"Not yet," said Mr. Pricklepants. "But you can make it so. You've got to *believe* it to *be* it!"

He placed a muddy paw on Rex's cheek and gave him the clan's mark of bravery.

On top of the volcano, Buzz tried to lure the giant dinosaur closer to the edge.

Suddenly, the King of the Jungle dangled the Alien over the volcano's **fiery** opening. Rex had to do something!

RRRROOOO

"Leave my friends alone!" cried Rex. Then he took a deep breath and began to grow.

Rex let out **roar** after **roar,** each one louder and stronger than the one before it. He grew bigger and bigger with every roar!

RRRRROO

Soon Rex was towering over the King of the Jungle.
Rex let out his biggest, baddest **roar** yet. It echoed
through the jungle. It shook the trees. It rattled the ground.
And it frightened the King of the Jungle.

"Now!" called Woody. He threw his rope across the volcano's opening, causing the frightened dinosaur to trip.

Buzz quickly swooped in and grabbed the Alien from the dinosaur's claws. Then Rex let out one last **roar** and the King of the Jungle fell into the volcano!

AARRR

Rex's friends began to clap and cheer.
"Our hero!" called the cave-Aliens.
"Hooray for the new King of the Jungle!"
said Mr. Pricklepants.
Rex let out a **roar** of excitement, causing
his friends to cheer even louder. He roared
and roared . . .

. . . until he woke up, surrounded by all his friends. The jungle had been a dream—and Rex had been roaring in his sleep!

"That was the best **roar** I've ever heard!" said Mr. Pricklepants. "The role is yours!"

Rex might not have been in the jungle anymore, but he sure felt like a king.